Four Friends
AT
Christmas

For Anne Taylor Davis, who says,
"Christmas dinner is all about
the brussels sprouts."
—T DEP

SIMON & SCHUSTER BOOKS FOR YOUNG READERS
An imprint of Simon & Schuster Children's Publishing Division
1230 Avenue of the Americas, New York, New York 10020

Book design by Paula Winicur
The text for this book is set in Celestia Antiqua.
Printed in Hong Kong

2 4 6 8 10 9 7 5 3 1

Library of Congress Cataloging-in-Publication Data
De Paola, Tomie.
Four friends at Christmas / Tomie de Paola
p. cm.
Summary: Mister Frog is usually asleep at Christmas time,
but this year his good friends make sure that he has a wonderful holiday.
ISBN 0-689-85282-7
[1. Christmas—Fiction. 2. Frogs—Fiction. 3. Animals—Fiction. 4. Friendship—Fiction.]
I. Title.
PZ7.D439 Fl 2002
[E]—dc21
2002021808

Four Friends at Christmas was previously published, in different form,
as the chapter entitled "Winter" in Four Stories for Four Seasons,
copyright © 1977 by Tomie dePaola

Four Friends
AT
Christmas

STORY AND PICTURES BY

Tomie dePaola

SIMON & SCHUSTER BOOKS FOR YOUNG READERS
New York London Toronto Sydney Singapore

It was wintertime and most animals were getting ready for the Christmas holidays, but some were getting ready for a long, long rest.

Mister Frog always slept right through the winter.

Most frogs do.

But, even though he always had a nice long rest and didn't have to bother with the snow and cold, he always missed Christmas. And Christmas always seemed such a joyous time of year.

His three friends told him how wonderful it was to celebrate the happy holiday.

"Oh, Froggy, you would love it! Turkey, plum pudding, candy canes, lots of good things to eat," said Mistress Pig.

"Candles, angels, and Christmas trees," said Missy Cat.

"Yule logs, Christmas carols, and Santa Claus," added Master Dog.

So Mister Frog decided to stay up and celebrate Christmas too.
He kept awake all through November.

By December first, Mister Frog was busy making Christmas lists, planning a Christmas dinner menu, writing out his Christmas cards and thinking about how he would decorate his house with holly and greens. And since Mister Frog had never had a Christmas before, he wanted everything to be absolutely perfect.

Mister Frog couldn't believe how exciting Christmastime was, but after all his planning and list-making he was very tired.

"Christmas is a lot of work!" thought Mister Frog. "I think I'll just take a tiny nap here on the couch before I go to the store," he said.

Mister Frog had a nice long nap. And it was just what he needed for a busy day of shopping. But when the church bells rang out, ding, dong, ding, dong, ding, dong, Mister Frog jumped up with a start.

"Goodness," croaked Mister Frog, "I hope I haven't overslept." But he had.

There were no turkeys left, no cranberries, no candy canes, no Christmas wreaths.

In fact, all the stores were closed.

Mister Frog couldn't even find a Christmas tree. And it was Christmas Eve.

Poor Froggy!

Mister Frog couldn't believe he had missed Christmas again. All of his hard work had been for nothing. Now he had no Christmas dinner, no Christmas decorations, and no Christmas tree. As he sat alone in his house, Mister Frog wondered if his three best friends were celebrating Christmas. All of a sudden the doorbell rang ding-a-ling and Mr. Frog went to see who was there.

"Ho, ho, ho, merry Christmas," said Santa Claus.

Mister Frog was shocked. Santa Claus had just arrived at his house with a beautiful Christmas tree just for him!

He invited Santa Claus inside and was just about to say thank you, when the doorbell rang again.

Ding-a-ling.

"Ho, ho, ho, merry Christmas," said Santa Claus.

Mister Frog couldn't believe his eyes. There at the door, was *another* Santa Claus with *another* Christmas tree just for him.

Mister Frog invited the second Santa Claus in and was about to shut the door when the bell rang *again!*

Ding-a-ling.

"Ho, ho, ho, merry Christmas," said Santa Claus.

Mister Frog opened the door and there was a *third* Santa Claus with a *third* Christmas tree just for him.

"Merry Christmas, merry Christmas, merry Christmas," Mister Frog said to each Santa.

"And surprise, surprise, surprise," said Missy Cat, Master Dog, and Mistress Pig, taking off their Santa hats and beards.

Mister Frog couldn't believe it. The three mystery Santas were actually his three best friends coming to wish him a merry Christmas.

"Let's hang up our stockings," said Master Dog.

"Here's the plum pudding!" said Mistress Pig.

"And we four friends are all celebrating Christmas together," said Missy Cat.

"This is the best Christmas ever," said Mister Frog as he
gathered around his three friends and his three Christmas trees.

Then all four friends began to sing:

"Silent night, holy night,

All is calm, all is bright . . ."

And because Mister Frog was there this time, it was indeed the best Christmas ever.